REMY SNEAKERS
VS. THE ROBO-RATS

KEVIN SHERRY

SCHOLASTIC PRESS / NEW YORK

Dedicated to all the cool librarians out there. The best and most fun classroom is the school library.

Library of Congress Cataloging-in-Publication Data

Names: Sherry, Kevin, author, illustrator. | Title: Remy Sneakers vs. the Robo-Rats / by Kevin Sherry. | Description: First edition. | New York : Scholastic Press, 2017. | Summary: There has been a break in at the Science Museum, and the chief suspect is Remington Raccoon, commonly known as Remy Sneakers, so with the help of Stix the mouse and other city critters, Remy sets out to discover the truth—and the Critter Crew finds themselves up against a criminal mastermind and his army of robo-rodents. | Identifiers: LCCN 2016040573 | ISBN 9781338034608 (hardcover) | Subjects: LCSH: Raccoon—Comic books, strips, etc. | Raccoon—Juvenile fiction. | Mice—Comic books, strips, etc. | Mice—Juvenile fiction. | Animals—Comic books, strips, etc. | Animals—Juvenile fiction. | Robots—Comic books, strips, etc. | Robots—Juvenile fiction. | CYAC: Graphic novels. | Humorous stories. | Raccoon—Fiction. | Mice—Fiction. | Animals—Fiction. | Robots—Fiction. | LCGFT: Graphic novels. | Humorous fiction. | Classification: LCC PZ7.7.S468 Re 2017 | DDC 741.5/973—dc23 | LC record available at https://lccn.loc.gov/2016040573

10 9 8 7 6 5 4 3 2 1   17 18 19 20 21

Printed in the U.S.A. 23

First edition, May 2017

Book design by Carol Ly

Chapter 1

A SNEAKY CRIME

Trouble was brewing for
Remy Sneakers...

CiTy NEWS

50¢

BREAK-IN at the MUSEUM!

Last night, valuable pieces of high-tech lightweight metal were stolen from the Air & Space Museum.

Witnesses say the thief was a raccoon.

2

I don't understand. Stix, where did you get this?

It's today's newspaper.

And people are saying the story is about you. You didn't do it, right, Remy?

Please tell me you're not the thief...

3

Of course not. I may like to collect things, but I would never steal. Especially from a museum.

CITY NEWS 50¢

BREAK-IN at the MUSEUM!

Last night, valuable pieces of high-tech lightweight metal were stolen from the Air & Space Museum.

Witnesses say the thief

4

Sigh.

Don't believe
everything you read.

I bet you're not the only one
who thinks that I'm the thief.
I have to figure out who
did this. It's the only way to
clear my name.

And what IS my name, you ask? It's **Remington Raccoon,** but everyone calls me

Remy Sneakers!

POTTED CACTI

BUG LARVAE SHELLS

LOBSTER CLAW

WHALE VERTEBRAE

TRICYCLE

I'm a collector.

WIGS

HAMMOCK

SUNGLASS COLLECTION

POWERFUL MAGNETS

WINTER HAT COLLECTION

ZIPLINE

INNER TUBES

ROLLER SKATES

OLD CAMERAS

PEBBLES THAT LOOK LIKE HEADS

SAND FROM OCEAN CITY IN A JAR

The best things I've ever found were these **awesome little sneakers**. All it took to make them new again was some tender loving care...

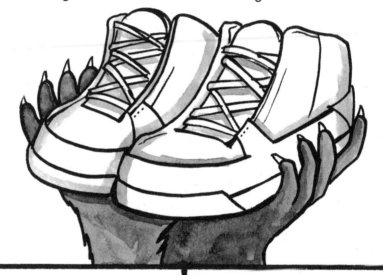

...and some thread.

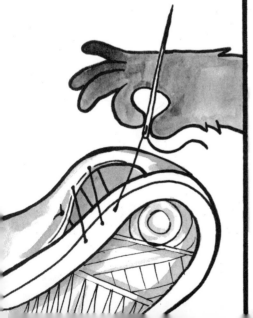

Now I have the freshest sneakers in the whole city

I'm famous all over town for these bad boys.

I'm also known for my collection.

Some call the stuff I find weird. Some call it trash. But I call it treasure.

Remy is kind of my hero.

9

I would never resort to stealing

10

to add to my collection.

I knew in my heart you weren't
the thief. But my fellow mice have
been wondering, so I had to ask.

Do you think they will help me find the real thief?

I don't know about the others, but I'm pretty sure my sisters will help.

TOY SHOP

Chapter 2
MOUSEVILLE

MICE OF MOUSEVILLE

It seemed Remy's word was not enough to convince the mice.

Wow! Tough crowd!

Look!
It's my sisters Trixie and Pixie.

19

My favorite sisters. Pixie, Trixie, we need your help! Remy has been falsely accused of burglary. But he didn't do it. We are going to prove that he's innocent.

Our favorite brother! And that's saying a lot, since we have hundreds of siblings.

Of course we will help you, Stix! If you say Remy didn't do it, we believe you.

We should ask the rats for help. They may be a little difficult to work with, but they are also crafty and clever.

Chapter 3
RAT CITY

It's easy to find the entrance to Rat City. You can smell this greasy restaurant from a mile away.

DOWN here!

Rat City was a *long* way from Remy's peaceful tower.

TRAINING RING

CASE OF TWINKLES

CASE OF YUMMYKAKES

CASE OF CHOCOLATE COOKIES

"BORROWED"
FLAT SCREEN TV

BOOTLEGGED ELECTRICITY

"THE THRONE"

CUDDLE PILE

Hey there, rat buddies!

I was wondering if I could ask you an important question.

Hold it right there! We don't like thieves in Rat City.

Look what we have here—a raccoon in Rat City! I hear the famous Remington Raccoon is asking for our help!

I **know** just the rat for the job.

But that means... you'll owe us one.

All right, I guess.

Torch, you're going to accompany our friend Remington on his very important mission.

If I have to escort you helpless critters, we're gonna do things my way. Now, hurry up.

Stix could not know that toy maker Walter Fry was trouble with a capital T.

Mayor Spike wants to find the "thief" with help from citizens like me?

/ It's time for my toy army to go to work.

If only she knew what they can really do!

Here we are.

HEY, PIGEONS!

It's me, Torch. We need your help. Will you talk?

PIGEONS OF PIGEON PLAZA

Hi, Patty. I guess you knew we were coming...

Pigeons are the eyes in the sky. We see everything that goes on around here.

And it looks like you, Remington, **are a criminal!**

The Critter Crew was lost.
They didn't have any clues.

And no help
was on the way.

An explosion blasted a nearby hardware store.

And the Critter Crew spotted a raccoon-shaped shadow leaving with a sack of stolen goods!

But when Remy got a good look at the thief, it was no raccoon.

It was a robot!

A robot that looked just like Remy.

He had the same pointy ears, the same nimble fingers, and the same awesome sneakers. Only the robo-raccoon was made of metal and had Terminator vision.

<:// STATUS:::FRAMED:::SCAPEGOAT:::PATSY

Before Remy could grab him, the robo-raccoon sprinted down the street.

Chapter 5

WALTER'S PLAN

Welcome, Remington Raccoon, my favorite muse!

I see you've met my light-fingered robotic friend.

But, then, that was all part of my plan.

I've been making toys for years.
But my real passion is spying! And I have an idea
that will change everything for this town.

But I didn't have the money or supplies I needed to make
my dreams come true. So I decided to build myself a thief.
And you, Remington Raccoon, were the perfect model.

The robo-raccoon has helped me steal everything I need to save this city. And it was easy to pin it all on you!

Not so fast!

My Critter Crew will stop you! After all, there are only two of you and five of us.

Let's get out of here!

Guys, we need all the help we can get if we are going to defeat this gang of robo-rodents. We're going to have to go back to the mice, rats, and pigeons and try to convince them to join our crew. In the past, we all kept to ourselves. We tolerated one another. But now is the time to work together!

All the city critters must unite!

It's the only way to stop Walter and expose the real criminal here!

The mice quickly joined Remy's cause.

But the rats were a little harder to convince

If you let Walter win, Rat City will never be the same...

PLANS

58

You should have seen it! He had a whole building full of creepy little rodent robots. We need your toughness to beat them.

And the pigeons wouldn't even talk!

But Remy could not wait for the pigeons to come around. He needed to devise a battle plan.

we know this city better than anyone!

PLANS

The Critter Crew gathered all the tools they could find.

SCREWDRIVER

FORK

MARBLES

Mice and rats worked together for the first time in history.

Even the rat king got into the spirit.

Why don't we sing the Critter Crew song?

We don't know
    but we've been told
City Critters are mighty bold.
We may be rough,
    we may be tough,
But this town is ours...
And we've had enough!

Chapter 6

SHOWDOWN IN THE STREETS

The Critter Crew
was finally ready
to rumble!

They marched into the toy shop, ready for action.

I couldn't defeat you before...

And I
brought a few
friends with me!

Walter did not look scared.

My toy army was designed for this.

But when the marbles fell, so did the robots.

The mice tied them in knots.

And the magnets stopped them in their tracks.

Hey, Remy!

These toys are no match for real rodents!

An unstoppable squad of

TITANIUM-PLATED

PIGEON SPY

DRONES!

73

You see, I built the robo-raccoon to steal the materials I needed to make the drones and the money I needed to take online courses in advanced robotics.

Fall back!

What have I done?

I was so worried about my reputation that I got us into this gigantic mess. I'm trying my best, but that might not be good enough. And if we can't stop Walter's drones, he'll spy on the whole city. No one will be safe. He'll keep stealing and spying until he controls everything.

What are we going
to do now?

Walter has my back up
against the wall...

FLUTTER

The pigeons are here to help!

In the past, we minded our own beeswax. But now that these criminals are invading our space, we can't perch on the sidelines any longer. It's our turn to join the fight!

Soon the news of the battle of the beasts was everywhere.

Chapter 7

MAYOR SHEILA SPIKE

Hello? Channel 3 News?

Yes, I have a moment. Now just calm down
and explain to me what is going on...

It's chaos down at the toy shop!
Our city is facing a perfect storm of rodent rage as mice and rats and pigeons clash in the streets.
Some of these vermin are all fur and feathers. But others appear to be robots, including a metal raccoon wearing sneakers! Sounds a lot like your mysterious thief, no?
Store owner Walter Fry seems to have created the brawling bots. From all his shouting, it seems the pigeon drones were quite valuable tools he's been using to spy on the city.
Care to comment?

Mayor Spike could not believe her ears.
When she asked citizens to help her catch the thief,
this wasn't exactly what she'd had in mind!

We've got to get down to the toy shop now!

I hope this doesn't affect my chances at reelection...

MAYOR

Chapter 8

REMY'S REVENGE

Meanwhile, Remy snuck back into the toy shop.

If I can disable Walter's computer, maybe I can stop these dreadful drones!

I just have to type

CANCEL

and those foul fowl will drop out of the sky!

But just as Remy's little fingers trembled over the keys...

I still have a few tricks up my robo-sleeve. I have escaped your ropes and evaded your friends.

And now I am going to end you!

The robo-raccoon had
Remy trapped.

And he was about to lock the
program that would keep the pigeon
drones flying forever when...

The critters from Pigeon Plaza . . .

. . . had not taken off at the first sign of trouble!

We were wrong about you, Remy.

But we won't let you down this time!

Robots are no match for the power of friendship.

CANCEL
ABORT
STOP
ARREST

With his nimble raccoon fingers, Remy canceled the pigeon drone operation.

JUSTICE FOR ALL

My pigeon drones are ruined.
They were supposed to make me rich and powerful.
Oh, my poor babies...

TOY SHOP

Come on, Critter Crew! Let's not get in the mayor's way. It looks like Walter is about to get what's coming to him!

This is a nightmare!

That harebrained toy maker almost took down the whole city.

Arrest him!

I made these drones for you, Mayor! You asked citizens to help catch the thief. This was really your idea...

Don't you try to trick me, Walter.
What about your robo-raccoon? Did you think
I wouldn't find out? You were behind the
robberies AND the pigeon spies.

Friends, rodents, critters, lend me your ears. That means listen up! We just did something huge! We found the real criminal, beat him and his evil robots, and cleared my name. We proved that critters belong in this city.

And we did it side-by-side. We may all be different, but when we work together, there is nothing we can't do! Now let's all go home.
A talking raccoon? This is an even bigger story!
3

Remy, I'm sorry we didn't listen to you sooner.
I guess we have some trust issues. But we'll work on them, because now we know we have each other's backs.

Why don't you guys come back to my crib for tea and cookies?

Remy didn't know it, but a nasty surprise was waiting for him...

Everything I love is lost,
stolen, or broken.

And my tower—
it's destroyed!

TANGLED WIGS

RIPPED
HAMMOCK

BROKEN
SUNGLASSES

FLAT INNER TUBES

MORE EMPTY SHELVES

SPILLED
SAND

119

First I was framed, then I was trounced by robo-rats, and now the collection I've been working on my whole life is ruined. It's almost enough to make a raccoon give up.

Remy, you are a great leader and a great friend. You brought us city critters together. And you taught us that when we work together, we can accomplish great things.

...but I do!

TO BE CONTINUED...

ABOUT THE AUTHOR

Kevin Sherry is the author and illustrator of many children's books, most notably The Yeti Files series and *I'm the Biggest Thing in the Ocean*, which received starred reviews and won an original artwork award from the Society of Illustrators. He's a man of many interests: a chef, a cyclist, an avid screen printer, and a performer of hilarious puppet shows for kids and adults. Kevin lives in Baltimore, Maryland.

ACKNOWLEDGMENTS

Thanks to Teresa Kietlinski, Madeline Tess Peters, Kelly LaSerre, Erin Nutsugah, my brother, Brian, and to my mom and dad.

ALSO BY KEVIN SHERRY: